MAISIE AND THE SPACE INVADER

Author and Illustrator: Aileen Paterson

This story is dedicated to Jerry Vanderbilt-Sloane
With thanks to Mrs Kay Johnston

© Aileen Paterson

Published in 1988 by
The Amaising Publishing House Ltd.
Musselburgh
EH21 7UJ
Scotland

031-665 8237

Reprinted 1993
Printed & Bound by Scotprint Ltd, Musselburgh

ISBN 1 871512 02 6

Other Maisie Titles in the Series:

It was a fine breezy April morning, perfect for drying washing and blowing cobwebs away. Maisie's Granny felt as happy as a lark, even though she'd been up since dawn, beating carpets and mopping floors.

Now she stood at the kitchen sink washing her lace curtains, singing along with Radio Morningside.

Granny's singing, and the thunder of the washing machine spinning, woke Maisie. When she went into the kitchen, still half-asleep, her eyes soon opened wide. The place was in a real fankle. Clouds of steam filled the air, sheets and curtains lay on the table, and a strong smell of soap and polish tickled her nose. She tugged at Granny's apron strings.

"Good morning, Maisie," beamed Granny. "Isn't this a lovely day for my Spring-cleaning?

The rain's stopped at last.

Wait now and I'll get you some breakfast."

She wiped her paws on her pinny and fetched a mug of milk and a plate of toast. No porridge and no kippers today.

Maisie's face fell.

She was a kitten who enjoyed her food, but Granny was too busy to notice. She plunged her paws into the sink again, and chirruped,

"Maisie, Maisie, give me your answer do,
I'm half crazy all for the love of you . . ."

After breakfast, Maisie decided to escape from the hubbub. None of her friends were up yet, so she fetched her football and went down to the back green to practice goal kicks.

Archie her best friend, had been teaching her some of the finer points of the game.

A few minutes later someone else came into the back green— someone else who was spring cleaning too.

It was Mrs McKitty, Granny's perjink neighbour, carrying a big basket of snow-white washing.

As soon as she saw Maisie and the football, she ordered her out.

"Maisie MacKenzie! This is a drying-green, not a football pitch!

Off you go upstairs to your Granny!"

Maisie put out a paw to take her ball, but Mrs McKitty swept it up and silently pointed to the back door.

Maisie fled upstairs.

She tiptoed into her bedroom and shut the door. What a dreadful day so far. No porridge, no kippers, and now no football.

She sat on the window seat and looked out. Down below, the washing was waving in the breeze, but there was no sign of Mrs McKitty. She had gone indoors to chase away any specks of dust that had dared to enter her flat.

Maisie began to write a letter to her Daddy, far away exploring up the Amazon. It is just as well that this letter was never finished, for it was just a list of grumbles, but something happened which put all her complaints out of her head!

Outside the window something seemed to be blocking the light. Maisie glanced up. A huge shiny soap-bubble was drifting by, bigger by far than any kitten ever blew. Maisie was puzzled.

Where had it come from?

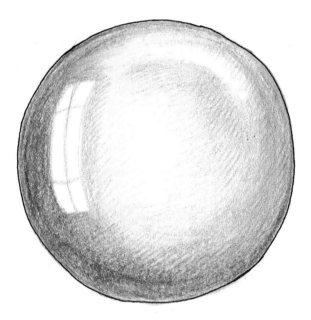

Could it have blown out of Granny's kitchen window?

She stood up to watch it whirling lower and lower, down towards the back green. Then an amazing thing happened! When it landed on top of the washing line, the rope snapped with a loud crack, and bubble and washing tumbled to the ground!

Maisie gasped.

The bubble hadn't popped—as bubbles always do.

What could it mean?

She suddenly remembered Mrs McKitty's stern warning and somehow she knew she would get the blame for the fallen washing but, like all kittens, she was full of curiosity, and now it got the better of her.

Downstairs she flew, as fast as her little paws would carry her, and out on to the grass where the bubble lay.

It was a beautiful sight—all the colours of the rainbow and sparkling in the sun, but Maisie felt a bit afraid now that she was near. She stretched out her paw timidly, and tapped it with her claws. The bubble didn't burst! Her fur rose up in fright, and her whiskers tingled—from inside the bubble, someone or something was tapping back.

Before she could run away to the safety of Granny, a door opened in the side of the bubble, and a kitten popped his head out. Maisie's legs turned to jelly.

THIS WAS NO ORDINARY KITTEN!

For a start—he was bright green, and on top of his head was a tuft of pink fur. He was dressed in a silver suit, and he stared at Maisie with large golden eyes. Then he smiled, and she knew that everything was going to be all right. He spoke in a tinkling voice.

"Greetings. My name is Meeno, and I come from Planet Pluto in the seventh galaxy. What is your name please, and where am I?"

"My name is Maisie, and you've landed in my back green," she answered, fairly quivering with excitement now.

He was a space kitten!

Meeno looked puzzled—back greens are not a feature of the landscape on Pluto.

So Maisie began again.

"This is Edinburgh—the capital of Scotland," she announced proudly.

"Aha," said Meeno, "So you are an Earth-kitten! I didn't mean to come quite so far. I'm only a learner driver, you see, and sometimes I press the wrong button. Now, Maisie, take me to your Leader."

"I haven't got one of those," said Maisie, "Will a Granny do?" Meeno nodded and jumped down beside her.

But upstairs, trouble was brewing. Just before Maisie's arrival on the scene, Mrs McKitty had glanced out of her window and, although she wasn't wearing her glasses, she saw enough to give her a nasty shock. She rushed next door to Granny, waving her sweeping-brush.

"Quick, Isabella," she shouted, "Fetch your mop. Someone's invaded the back green and vandalised my washing. The rope's broken, and my best sheets and towels have been thrown on the grass. It must be those terrible MacTuff kittens that sprayed their names in the close. We've got to catch them."

Greatly alarmed, Granny followed her friend downstairs. The MacTuff brothers were newcomers and already infamous as bullies and bad-cats.

They rushed out on to the grass, then drew up, panting, in front of Maisie. The Space Kitten jumped back inside his spaceship, and peeped out at them all. Poor Granny was totally confused. There was no sign of the MacTuffs, but what was Maisie doing there?

What was that big bubble in the middle of the washing, and who was the little stranger?

She couldn't take it all in. But Mrs McKitty's dander was up. Maisie had struck again.

"This is outrageous," she squawked. "Maisie MacKenzie, you were warned not to play out here. What's been going on? I demand an explanation!"

Before Maisie could give her one, Mrs McKitty had turned towards the kitten.

"As for you," she said, "that object will have to be removed at once. I don't know where you come from, but this is Morningside, and we don't allow ruffians here. I've got a good mind to send for the police."

"Oh please don't do that," wailed Maisie, "He's not a ruffian. His name is Meeno, and he's a—a Plutonian. That's his spaceship! He didn't mean to land on your washing, but he's not very good at steering yet."

Mrs McKitty snorted, dismissing it all as more of Maisie's nonsense.

Granny had been looking inside the bubble.

"Come and see this, Marjorie," she said.

From the doorway they could see a computer, star-maps, and lots of buttons and switches.

Mrs McKitty went quiet.

Granny spoke up.

"We'd better not send for the police. They might arrest the wee soul for dangerous driving, and then he'll never get home. Let's all go upstairs and have a cup of tea."

And, taking charge, she helped Meeno down and led the way out of the back green. Maisie fetched her friends Archie, Hector, Effie and Flora, and together they picked up the scattered washing, pushed the spaceship into the safety of the shed, then rushed up to Granny's kitchen.

Granny passed round tea and milk and scones.
"Eat up, Meeno," she said, "You're at your Aunty's."

But Meeno didn't like Earth food. Mrs McKitty fetched some of her famous Millionaire's Shortbread, but he wouldn't touch it. She was black-affronted!

All the kittens began asking Meeno questions, but he jumped off his stool and said,
"I'd like to see Edinburgh, please, before I go home. May the kittens show me round?"

It seemed a good idea. Maisie could get Granny's messages while they were out, and Granny and Mrs McKitty could finish their work.

So off they went, on the 23 bus, to see the sights of Edinburgh.

As the bus took them into the city, Meeno told them about his Planet and his family.

Pluto sounded wonderful. The weather was always warm and sunny, the buildings were made of the same pretty stuff as the bubble, and every cat had his own spaceship. His Mummy and Daddy were Star Fleet pilots! The kittens were greatly impressed.

They discovered that he knew a lot about things like electronics and science, but he didn't know very much about Scotland.

He'd never heard of Auchtermuchty or Penny Chews or Pipe Bands or jeely pieces. He'd never heard of the greatest football team in the world—Archie's team—Heart of Midlothian.

He'd never even heard of FOOTBALL!

"That's terrible," gasped Archie, "We must give you a game before you go home."

Maisie discovered that there were no sweetie shops on Pluto. Life must be very dreich without a piece of tablet now and then. There's no place like home, she thought—but Meeno thought the same.

He wasn't very impressed by Edinburgh. He said the castle was too old and grey, and he didn't like the noise and smell of the traffic in Princes Street, so different from Pluto's clean, fast spacecraft.

Effie suggested a trip to the Zoo, but Flora said it was too risky. They might keep Meeno there as a specimen and put him in a cage that said "DO NOT FEED".

Meeno was horrified when he heard this.

He thought Edinburgh was awful, and besides, he was feeling very hungry.

Luckily, Maisie had a brainwave.

"There's a nice shop in Leith that sells all kinds of foreign food, and you're a foreigner. They must have something there you'd like to eat and I can buy Granny's messages."

So off they went before Meeno could say another word.

There was a delicious smell of coffee and salami and fresh bread inside the shop and the cat serving behind the counter was serenading the queue.

When it was Maisie's turn, he sang a song to her.

> Buy my Spaghetti
> For your husband's tea—
> It makes Cats sing Good
> In I T A L E E!

"Try a sample of my lovely cheese, Signorina Maisie," he cried, handing her down a basket.

Now this cheese was very strong stuff. The smell made Maisie's eyes water. Her nose twitched so she covered it with her paw. The kittens gasped and coughed. But Meeno began to purr. He reached out his paw, popped a piece in his mouth, then he smiled.

He LIKED it!

"This is better than Martian marmalade or Plutonian pancakes! Edinburgh isn't too bad!" he said cheerily.

Maisie bought a whole pound of the cheese, and Meeno nibbled it all the way to Morningside on the bus, while Archie explained the game of Football to him.

He wanted to organise a match before Meeno returned to Pluto.

When they got to Morningside Mansions, Archie and Hector went off to collect their football strips. Maisie, Meeno, Flora and Effie walked on towards Granny's close.

Suddenly, Maisie stopped in alarm.

The MacTuffs were coming towards them!

Quick as a flash, Maisie opened her message bag and told Meeno to jump in. He was puzzled, but he did as she asked.

The MacTuffs drew up in front of them and blocked their way.

"What's in your bag, Maisie," demanded Billy MacTuff in his gruff growly voice.

"Any sweeties in there?" enquired his brother, in his squeaky, spluttery voice.

Maisie was too frightened to answer and tried to dodge out of their way as they pulled at the bag. Effie squealed with terror and hid behind Flora. The MacTuffs grabbed the bag from Maisie's paws, and emptied it on to the pavement!

Out tumbled Meeno, looking very cross and very fierce . . .
"You'd better STOP it," he shouted.
"Who says so?" sneered the MacTuffs.
"I do." said Meeno.

Well, when they looked down at this tiny wee green warrior facing up to THEM, "The Great MacTuffs", they exploded into laughter. The tears rolled down their cheeks so fast that they didn't notice Meeno putting his paw into his pocket. He had some magic stardust with him in case of trouble. He pulled out a big pawful and flung it all over them!
The laughter stopped.
The MacTuffs stood as still as statues.

Maisie and the others didn't wait to see what happened next. They picked up Meeno, bag and all, and ran upstairs to Granny's kitchen.

They were busy telling Granny all about their adventures when Mrs McKitty arrived in from the shops, looking very puzzled.

"You'll never believe what's just happened," she announced. "Billy and Andy MacTuff helped me across the road, and carried my shopping up the stairs for me. I can't imagine what's come over them!"

But Maisie, Effie and Flora could.

Next minute, Archie and Hector arrived and announced to Granny and Mrs McKitty, their plans for a game of Football in the back green. Granny smiled, and said she thought it was a grand idea but, of course, Mrs McKitty would have none of it.

Maisie's football had been confiscated for this kind of thing, her washing had been ruined—quite enough for one day. There was no persuading her.

Meeno was disappointed, he wanted so much to try this strange game.

He felt in his pocket, there was still a little stardust left, enough to transform Mrs McKitty for an hour or so.

He pulled it out quietly and threw it over her.

A strange blue light filled the room.

Mrs McKitty began to smile and chuckle at everyone.

Then she spoke.

"A game of football on the back green, did you say? What a splendid idea. I'll be goalie if you like! I was quite an athlete in my youth, you know."

She ran next door with a skip and a hop, and fetched Maisie's ball. The kittens were astonished, this was real magic.

Granny was a bit worried, but Meeno assured her that there were no ill effects.

It was an historic event. Granny played in Goal for Maisie, Flora and Effie, while Mrs McKitty was goalkeeper for Archie, Hector and Meeno.

Meeno loved every minute of it.

His footwork was first-class and he headed the ball with the pink tuft on the top of his head. Granny was no match for him. He scored three goals for his team.

Maisie managed to get one past Mrs McKitty, who tried valiantly to save it.

Meeno's team won in the end.

Granny took a photograph of them with her instant camera, for Meeno to take home.

It was time for him to go, for he knew his family must be getting worried. He thanked everyone for being so kind, and said he'd had a lovely time in Scotland.

The kittens helped him to push the bubble out of the shed.

Mrs McKitty gave him a Scottish flag, and the kittens gave him the football so he could teach his friends on Pluto.

He climbed aboard, and pressed the starter.

The spaceship rose into the air.

Meeno waved his flag and his new friends waved back until he was far above them.

Then they noticed that the Edinburgh sky was filled with a fleet of bubbles. They had come to escort Meeno safely home.

One by one they disappeared from sight . . . as bubbles always do.

The kittens felt both sad and happy. Granny and Mrs McKitty went indoors for a cup of tea. It had been a long and exciting day for everyone.

In no time at all Mrs McKitty was her usual self. She seemed to have forgotten the football match, though she did complain of a stiff back and sore joints for a few days.

"I'm shattered to fragments—I must have overdone it with my spring-cleaning this year," she told Granny.

The MacTuffs did not return to their old selves. They joined the Scouts and the Sunday School!

Peace returned to Morningside.

Maisie told the whole story in a long and happy letter to Daddy.

"Dear Daddy," she began, "I've got lots of exciting news for you. You're never going to believe it. Mrs McKitty played football in the back green—but I'd better begin from the beginning . . .!"

Glossary

back green	communal back garden
black-affronted	embarrassed
close	corridor, alley
dreich	dull, dreary
fankle	disorder
jeely pieces	jam sandwiches
millionaire's shortbread	slice of shortbread topped by caramel and chocolate
penny chews	caramel toffees
perjink	excessively neat
pinny	pinafore (apron)
tablet	fudge

The Song of The MacTuffs

(One has gruff voice, One has high splashy voice—like "Sausages is the Boys")

We're worse than Dennis The Menace
Worse than Attila The Hun
We hide up closes, then pounce on wee kittens
Pinch all their sweeties and run—
That's what we call having FUN!

We're no sissies, we're ROTTEN
We spray our names on the stair
And when Mrs McKitty asks "Who made this Mess?"—
We say, "It wisnae us, it was Them over there"
That's what we call Playing Fair.